BISCUITS & SLICES

Photography by Peter Barry
Designed by Richard Hawke and Claire Leighton
Edited by Jillian Stewart and Kate Cranshaw

3558
© 1993 Coombe Books
This edition published 1995 by Coombe Books for
Parragon Book Service Ltd
Unit 13-17 Avonbridge Trading Estate, Atlantic Road
Avonmouth, Bristol BS11 9QD
All rights reserved
Printed and bound in Hong Kong
ISBN 1-85813-472-2

BISCUITS & SLICES

PARRAGON

Contents

Introduction

There is nothing quite like home-baked biscuits and slices. Such a big business has been made out of biscuits and slices commercially, that most of us have forgotten how quick, simple and rewarding it is to make our own. Simple biscuits are something that anyone can make, even those who claim they can't cook.

The word 'biscuit' comes from old French 'bes cuit' which means twice cooked, and originally they had to be, for they were eaten on long sea voyages. There are three basic types of biscuit: rolled and moulded, drop and wafer, and sliced. Rolled and moulded biscuits – some of which are like a sweetened shortcrust pastry – are rolled out and cut with a pastry cutter, moulded into balls and flattened, or piped, so they don't spread during cooking. The finished texture can be soft and chewy or thin and crisp, depending on the recipe. Ordinary drop biscuits are the simplest type to make, with the mixture being dropped onto a baking sheet or spread out with a spoon, these biscuits do spread during cooking, so plenty of space must be left between them. The most delicate is the wafer biscuit, a type of drop biscuit made from very thin batter. The biscuits are often shaped or rolled up while they are still warm. Sliced biscuits, which are commonly known as slices or bars, are baked in a tin with the mixture being spread, poured or even pressed into it. The results can be cake-like, chewy or crumbly, depending on the recipe.

In *Biscuits and Slices*, there are recipes for everyday biscuits and cookies, such as Walnut Raisin Cookies, Shortbread Biscuits, and Ginger Nuts. For special occasions, or to accompany desserts, there are fancy biscuits such as Amaretti-Almond Macaroons, Langues de Chat, and Coconut Tile Cookies. For afternoon tea, choose from a selection of slices such as Cinnamon Almond Slices, or Pear and Apricot Slice, not forgetting all-time favourites such as Chocolate Brownies and Millionaires Shortbread. For an extra special treat, try Poppy Seed Slices, Praline Millefeuilles, or Continental Gateau Slices.

There are over fifty mouthwatering recipes in this book, some of which come from as far afield as America, Poland and Greece, so you will always be able to find something new to surprise and delight your family and friends. Quite a number of the biscuit recipes can be completed in about half an hour, and make a larger quantity than you would get in a bought packet, so next time you go to the supermarket, forget all the rows of biscuits and slices with their tempting packaging, and try making your own – the results will be a treat for everyone.

WALNUT RAISIN COOKIES

Home-made biscuits are a real treat. These are very quick and simple to make.

MAKES 36

225g/8oz butter
340g/12oz demerara sugar
3 eggs
1 tsp bicarbonate of soda dissolved in 1½
    tbsps hot water
370g/13oz flour
½ tsp salt
1 tsp cinnamon
120g/4oz walnuts, chopped
150g/5oz raisins

---

1. Cream the butter and sugar together until light and fluffy.

2. Beat in the eggs, one at a time.

3. Add the soda mixture, then work in half of the flour, together with the salt and cinnamon.

4. Mix in the walnuts and raisins, then the remaining flour.

5. Grease several baking trays and drop the mixture in spoonfuls about 2.5cm/1-inch apart.

6. Bake in an oven preheated to 180°C/350°F/Gas Mark 4, for about 8-10 minutes, or until golden brown.

7. Remove from the trays with a palette knife and cool on a wire rack.

TIME: Preparation takes about 15 minutes and cooking takes 8-10 minutes.

VARIATION: Use your favourite dried fruit and nuts to vary these cookies.

SHORTBREAD BISCUITS

Sandwich these biscuits together with raspberry jam for children's birthday parties.

MAKES ABOUT 18

150g/5oz plain flour
75g/2½oz light muscovado sugar, finely ground
120g/4oz butter, softened or soft margarine
½ tsp vanilla essence

1. Sieve the flour and sugar together and rub in the butter.

2. Add the vanilla essence and bind the mixture together.

3. Form into small balls and place on a baking tray about 7.5cm/3-inches apart.

4. With the back of a fork, press the balls down making a criss-cross pattern.

5. Bake in an oven preheated to 180°C/350°F/Gas Mark 4, for about 10-15 minutes until golden brown in colour.

6. Cool and store in an airtight container.

TIME: Preparation takes 10 minutes, cooking takes 10-15 minutes.

VARIATIONS: Add a tablespoon of currants to make fruit biscuits. Omit the vanilla essence and substitute almond essence to make almond biscuits.

PECAN PASTRIES

These sweet, nutty pastries are deep-fried to make them light and crisp.

MAKES 12

120g/4oz plain flour
1 tsp baking powder
¼ tsp salt
60ml/4 tbsps cold water
Oil for deep frying
280ml/½ pint golden syrup mixed with
    140ml/¼ pint treacle
90g/3oz pecans, finely chopped

---

1. Sift the flour, baking powder and salt together in a large bowl. Make a well in the centre and pour in the cold water.

2. Using a wooden spoon, mix until a stiff dough forms, and then knead by hand until smooth.

3. Divide the dough into 12 portions, each about the size of a walnut. Roll out each portion of dough on a floured surface into a very thin circle.

4. Heat the oil in a deep-fat fryer to 180°C/350°F. Drop each piece of pastry into the hot fat using two forks. Twist the pastry just as it hits the oil. Cook one at a time until light brown.

5. In a large saucepan, boil the syrup until it forms a soft ball when dropped into cold water. The soft-ball stage registers 115°C/239°F on a sugar thermometer.

6. Drain the pastries on kitchen paper after frying and dip carefully into the hot syrup. Sprinkle with pecans before the syrup sets and allow to cool before serving.

TIME: Preparation takes about 30 minutes and cooking takes about 2 minutes per pastry.

COOK'S TIP: The pastries must be served on the day they are made because they do not keep well.

VIENNESE FINGERS

These are lovely rich buttery biscuits with a hint of orange.

MAKES 12

175g/6oz butter or margarine
60g/2oz icing sugar
Grated zest of 1 orange
120g/4oz plain flour
60g/2oz cornflour

1. Cream together the butter, sugar and orange rind until fluffy. Sieve the flour and cornflour together and beat well into the mixture.

2. Spoon the mixture into a piping bag fitted with a 2.5cm/1-inch star nozzle and pipe 7.5cm/3-inch fingers, well separated, on a baking sheet lined with silicone paper.

3. Bake in an oven preheated to 180°C/350°F/Gas Mark 4, for 15 minutes. When cooked, transfer to a wire rack to cool.

TIME: Preparation takes 20 minutes and cooking takes 15 minutes.

SERVING IDEAS: Sandwich together with a little apricot jam.

CRULLERS

These crisp, light Polish biscuits are fried like fritters. They are best eaten on the day they are made and are lovely with coffee or tea.

MAKES 36

2 egg yolks
1 whole egg
60g/4 tbsps sugar
150g/5oz plain flour
Pinch salt
60ml/4 tbsps whipping cream
Icing sugar
Oil for deep frying

1. Beat yolks and whole egg together for about 10 minutes or until thick and pale in colour. Add the sugar and beat well. Sift the flour with a pinch of salt and whisk half of it into the egg mixture, alternating with the cream. Fold in the remaining flour. Leave to stand for 30 minutes in a cool place.

2. Turn the dough out onto a well-floured surface and knead with floured hands, the dough will be sticky at first.

3. Roll out very thinly with both a well-floured rolling pin and work surface.

4. Using a fluted pastry wheel, cut the dough into strips about 7.5×3.75cm/3×1½ inches.

5. Cut a slit in the centre of each piece.

6. Pull one end through the slit. Deep fry at 180°C/350°F for 3-4 minutes or until golden brown on both sides. Drain on kitchen paper and sprinkle with icing sugar before serving.

TIME: Prepration takes about 45 minutes and cooking takes about 3-4 minutes per batch.

SERVING IDEAS: Serve as an accompaniment to fruit or ice cream, or serve with coffee or tea.

PREPARATION: Cook a maximum of 6 crullers at a time.

SUSAN'S OATIES

For a super taste add finely chopped nuts or desiccated coconut to this recipe.

MAKES ABOUT 20 BISCUITS

120g/4oz butter or margarine
120g/4oz brown sugar
1 tsp molasses
1 tsp boiling water
1 tsp bicarbonate of soda
120g/4oz wholemeal flour
120g/4oz oats
½ tsp baking powder

1. Melt the butter, sugar and molasses in a saucepan.

2. Add the boiling water and bicarbonate of soda.

3. Remove from the heat and stir in the flour, oats and baking powder.

4. Place teaspoons of the mixture onto greased baking sheets.

5. Bake in an oven preheated to 160°C/325°F/Gas Mark 3, for 20 minutes.

6. Remove from the baking sheets and place on a wire tray to cool.

TIME: Preparation takes 10 minutes, cooking takes 20 minutes.

VARIATION: Use 60g/2oz oats and 60g/2oz desiccated coconut, but reduce the amount of sugar.

AMARETTI-ALMOND MACAROONS

Serve these delicious macaroons with tea or coffee.

MAKES ABOUT 24

225g/8oz whole almonds
225g/8oz granulated sugar
2 egg whites
1 tsp almond essence

1. Blanch the almonds by plunging them into boiling water for 2 minutes.

2. Skin the almonds and spread them over a baking sheet.

3. Dry off in a warm oven for a few minutes without browning.

4. Grind the granulated sugar until it resembles fine caster sugar.

5. Grind the almonds.

6. Sieve the sugar and almonds together.

7. In a large bowl, beat the egg whites until stiff but not dry.

8. Gradually fold in the almond and sugar mixture using a metal tablespoon, and add the almond essence.

9. Pipe or spoon the mixture onto a floured baking sheet, alternatively put the mixture on to sheets of rice paper.

10. Leave for as long as possible to rest before baking.

11. Bake in a preheated oven at 180°C/350°F/Gas Mark 4, for 15-20 minutes until golden brown.

12. Transfer the cooked macaroons to a cooling rack.

TIME: Preparation takes 15 minutes, cooking takes 15-20 minutes.

COOK'S TIP: The macaroons should be crisp on the outside but have a rather chewy centre. Longer cooking will crisp them all the way through if preferred.

SOUTHERN BISCUITS

In the Southern states of America, hot biscuits with butter are popular for breakfast, lunch, dinner or all three!

MAKES 6-8

200g/7oz plain flour
½ tsp salt
2 tsps baking powder
1 tsp sugar
½ tsp bicarbonate of soda
75g/2½oz butter or margarine
175ml/6 fl oz buttermilk

---

1. Sift the flour, salt, baking powder, sugar and bicarbonate of soda into a large bowl.

2. Rub in the butter until the mixture resembles coarse breadcrumbs.

3. Mix in enough buttermilk to form a soft dough. It may not be necessary to use all the buttermilk.

4. Turn the dough out onto a floured surface and knead lightly until smooth.

5. Roll the dough out on a floured surface to about 1.25-2cm/½-¾ inches thick. Cut into rounds with a 6.25cm/2½-inch pastry cutter.

6. Place the circles of dough on a lightly-greased baking sheet about 2.5cm/1-inch apart. Bake in a preheated 230°C/450°F/ Gas Mark 8 oven, for 10-12 minutes. Serve hot.

TIME: Preparation takes about 20 minutes and cooking takes about 10-12 minutes.

TO FREEZE: These biscuits freeze and reheat well. Freeze for up to 3 months and thaw at room temperature. To reheat, wrap in foil and place in a moderate oven for about 5 minutes.

GINGERBREAD MEN

These make wonderful biscuits for children's parties or for tea-time treats.

MAKES 18

225g/8oz plain flour
Pinch salt
2 tsps ground ginger
150g/5oz butter, in small pieces
1 egg, separated
30g/1oz caster sugar
2 tbsps treacle
Additional 30g/1oz caster sugar for glazing
Few currants

---

1. Sieve the flour, salt and ginger into a large mixing bowl. Add the butter and rub into the flour until the mixture resembles fine breadcrumbs.

2. Add the egg yolk, sugar and treacle, mix well, knead lightly and turn out onto a floured board.

3. Roll out to about 5mm/¼-inch thick and then cut out the gingerbread men (special cutters are easily available, or else let children cut out their own shapes).

4. Transfer them to greased baking sheets, brush with the egg white and sprinkle with the additional sugar. Press on the currants to form eyes and buttons.

5. Bake in an oven preheated to 180°C/350°F/Gas Mark 4, for 12-15 minutes, until golden brown. Allow to cool slightly before lifting off the baking sheets and placing them on wire racks.

TIME: Preparation takes about 20 minutes.
SERVING IDEAS: Decorate with white glacé icing.

PRALINES

A sugary, crunchy and thoroughly delectable confection with pecans. These are a favourite treat in the Bayou country and all over the southern states of America.

MAKES 12-16

340g/12oz unsalted butter
225g/8oz sugar
225g/8oz demerara sugar
225ml/8 fl oz milk
120ml/4 fl oz double cream
120g/4oz pecans, chopped
2 tsps vanilla or rum essence
1 tbsp water
Butter or oil

1. Melt the butter in a large, heavy-based pan. Add the sugars, milk and cream and bring mixture to the boil, stirring constantly.

2. Reduce the heat to simmering and cook to a deep golden brown syrup, stirring continuously. After about 20 minutes, drop a small amount of the mixture into iced water. If it forms a hard ball, the syrup is ready. The hard-ball stage registers 120°C/248°F on a sugar thermometer.

3. Add the pecans, flavouring and water. Stir until the mixture stops foaming. Grease baking sheets with butter or oil and drop on the mixture by spoonfuls, into mounds about 5cm/2 inches in diameter. The pralines will spread out as they cool. Allow to cool completely before serving.

TIME: Preparation takes about 25 minutes, and cooking takes about 20 minutes.

WATCHPOINT: When adding the flavourings and water, the mixture may spatter and can burn the skin. Add the liquid with a long-handled spoon or wear oven gloves.

VARIATION: Pralines are popular when made with sesame seeds, too. Add them in place of pecans.

BROWN SUGAR BISCUITS

*This rather thick dough bakes to a crisp golden brown – perfect as an
accompaniment to ice cream or fruit salad.*

MAKES ABOUT 36

275g/10oz light brown sugar
3 tbsps golden syrup
60ml/4 tbsps water
1 egg
250g/9oz plain flour
1 tbsp ground ginger
1 tbsp bicarbonate of soda
Pinch salt
120g/4oz finely chopped nuts

1. Mix the brown sugar, syrup, water and egg together in a large bowl. Beat with an electric mixer until light.

2. Sift flour with the ginger, bicarbonate of soda and salt into the brown sugar mixture and add the nuts. Stir by hand until thoroughly mixed.

3. Lightly oil three baking sheets and drop the mixture on, by spoonfuls, about 5cm/ 2-inches apart.

4. Bake in a preheated 190°C/375°F/Gas Mark 5 oven for about 10-12 minutes, or until lightly browned around the edges. Leave on the baking sheet for 1-2 minutes before removing with a palette knife to a wire rack to cool completely.

TIME: Preparation takes about 20 minutes and cooking takes about 10-12 minutes per batch.

VARIATION: Add raisins to the dough. Any variety of nuts will be good.

PREPARATION: The dough will keep in the refrigerator for several days. Allow to stand at room temperature for at least 15 minutes before using.

LEMON-ICED TREACLE COOKIES

Children in particular will love these colourful little biscuits.

MAKES ABOUT 30

120g/4oz butter or margarine
120g/4oz light muscovado sugar
1 egg, beaten
2 tbsps golden syrup
2 tsps baking powder
1 tsp ground allspice
½ tsp ground ginger
225g/8oz wholemeal flour
Pinch salt
460g/1lb icing sugar
Grated rind and juice of 1 lemon
Yellow food colouring (optional)
140ml/¼ pint water
Candied lemon slices (optional)

1. Beat together the butter and sugar until pale and creamy. Gradually add the egg, beating well after each addition.

2. Beat in the syrup, then using a metal spoon, fold in the baking powder, spices, flour and salt.

3. Place spoonfuls of the mixture on to two greased baking sheets and bake one tray at a time for 5-10 minutes in an oven preheated to 190°C/375°F/Gas Mark 5. Cool slightly on the tray then transfer to a wire rack to cool completely.

4. When all the biscuits are cooled, sieve the icing sugar into a bowl and add the lemon rind and juice. Add a little food colouring if using.

5. Gradually stir in enough of the water to form a thin coating icing and spread equal amounts onto each biscuit. Decorate if wished and allow icing to set before serving.

TIME: Preparation takes about 20 minutes, cooking time is about 30 minutes.

VARIATION: Use orange rind and juice in place of the lemon in this recipe.

HONEY SHORTBREAD

*Sweets in a honey syrup are quite common in Greece. Use hymettus honey, which
is dark and fragrant, for authenticity.*

340g/12oz plain flour, sifted
1 tsp baking powder
1 tsp bicarbonate of soda
280ml/½ pint olive oil
60g/2oz sugar
140ml/¼ pint brandy
60ml/4 tbsps orange juice
1 tbsp grated orange rind
60g/3oz walnuts, chopped
1 tsp cinnamon

Syrup
280ml/½ pint honey
120g/4oz sugar
280ml/½ pint water

1. Sift the flour, baking powder and
bicarbonate of soda together.

2. Combine the oil, sugar, brandy, orange
juice and rind in a large bowl or food
processor. Gradually add the sifted
ingredients, running the machine in short
bursts. Work just until the mixture comes
together.

3. Grease and flour several baking sheets.
Shape the shortbread mixture into ovals
about 7.5cm/3-inches long. Place well apart
on the prepared baking sheets and cook in
an oven preheated to 180°C/350°F/Gas
Mark 4, for about 20 minutes. Cool on the
baking sheets.

4. Mix the syrup ingredients together and
bring to the boil. Boil rapidly for 5 minutes
to thicken. Allow to cool.

5. Dip the cooled shortbread into the syrup
and sprinkle with the nuts and cinnamon.
Allow to set slightly before serving.

TIME: Preparation takes about 20 minutes, cooking takes 10 minutes for the
syrup to boil and about 20 minutes for the biscuits to bake.

TO FREEZE: Do not dip the biscuits in syrup. Wrap them well, label and
store for up to 2 months. Defrost thoroughly before coating with syrup, nuts
and cinnamon.

WATCHPOINT: If the mixture is overworked it becomes too soft to shape
and will spread when baked. Chill in the refrigerator to firm up.

ALMOND COOKIES

*In China these biscuits are often eaten as a between-meal snack. In Western style
cuisine, they make a good accompaniment to fruit or sorbet.*

MAKES 30 COOKIES

120g/4oz butter or margarine
60g/4 tbsps caster sugar
2 tbsps demerara sugar
1 egg, beaten
Almond essence
120g/4oz plain flour
1 tsp baking powder
Pinch salt
30g/1oz ground almonds, blanched or
    unblanched
30 whole blanched almonds
2 tbsps water

1. Cream the butter or margarine together
with the two sugars until light and fluffy.

2. Divide the beaten egg in half and add
half to the sugar mixture with a few drops
of the almond essence and beat until
smooth. Reserve the remaining egg for later
use. Sift the flour, baking powder and salt
into the egg mixture and add the ground
almonds. Stir well by hand.

3. Shape the mixture into small balls and
place well apart on a lightly greased baking
sheet. Flatten slightly and press an almond
on to the top of each one.

4. Mix the reserved egg with the water and
brush each biscuit before baking.

5. Place in a preheated 180°C/350°F/Gas
Mark 4 oven, and bake for 12-15 minutes.
The biscuits will be a pale golden colour
when done.

TIME: Preparation takes about 10 minutes. If the dough becomes too soft,
refrigerate for 10 minutes before shaping. Cooking takes about 12-15 minutes
per batch.

COOK'S TIP: Roll the mixture on a floured surface with floured hands to
prevent sticking.

WATCHPOINT: Do not over beat once the almonds are added. They will
begin to oil and the mixture will become too soft and sticky to shape.

SERVING IDEAS: Serve with fruit, ice cream or sorbet. Do not reserve just
for Chinese meals.

TO FREEZE: These may be frozen baked or unbaked. Defrost uncooked
dough completely at room temperature before baking. Baked biscuits may
be re-crisped by heating in the oven for about 2 minutes and then allowed
to cool before serving.

OATLET COOKIES

A delicious mix of oats, seeds and syrup make these cookies extra special.

MAKES 10 COOKIES

120g/4oz porridge oats
120g/4oz plain flour
90g/3oz sunflower seeds
30g/1oz sesame seeds
½ tsp mixed spice
120g/4oz butter or margarine
1 tbsp brown sugar
1 tsp golden syrup or molasses
½ tsp baking powder
1 tbsp boiling water
225g/8oz chocolate drops

1. Mix the oats, flour, sunflower seeds, sesame seeds and spice together.

2. Melt the butter, sugar and golden syrup or molasses over a gentle heat.

3. Add the baking powder and water to the syrup mixture and stir well.

4. Pour over dry ingredients and mix.

5. Place spoonfuls of the mixture well apart onto a greased baking tray and bake for 10 minutes in an oven preheated to 190°C/375°F/Gas Mark 5.

6. Allow to cool on the tray.

7. Melt the chocolate drops in a bowl over hot water and place teaspoonful of the melted chocolate on top of the cookies. Leave to set. Store in an airtight tin.

TIME: Preparation takes 15 minutes, cooking takes 10 minutes.

VARIATION: Ground ginger can be used in place of the mixed spice.

COOK'S TIP: Block chocolate may be used in place of the chocolate drops.

HERMITS

These are traditional American cookies, if you wish, you can include some chopped nuts and cinnamon for extra flavour.

MAKES ABOUT 50 COOKIES

120g/4oz butter
225g/8oz sugar
120ml/4 fl oz milk
225g/8oz flour
1 tsp allspice
½ tsp bicarbonate of soda
½ tsp cream of tartar
90g/3oz raisins

1. Cream the butter and sugar together until soft and fluffy, then gradually beat in the milk.

2. Sift together the flour, allspice, bicarbonate of soda and cream of tartar.

3. Add this to the butter mixture, beating well after each addition until the batter is smooth.

4. Chop the raisins, and stir them into the batter.

5. Drop teaspoonsful of the batter onto greased baking sheets, spacing them well apart.

6. Bake in an oven preheated to 190°C/375°F/Gas Mark 5, for 12-15 minutes.

7. Allow to cool slightly before removing the biscuits to a wire rack to cool completely.

TIME: Preparation takes about 15 minutes and cooking takes 12-15 minutes.

VARIATION: Substitute chopped mixed peel, sultanas or other dried fruit for the raisins.

BAKING POWDER BISCUITS

These American biscuits are very simple to make and taste delicious.

MAKES ABOUT 24 BISCUITS

225g/8oz flour
2 tsps baking powder
½ tsp salt
30g/1oz butter
225ml/8 fl oz milk

1. Sift the flour into a bowl together with the baking powder and salt. Rub in the butter. Add nearly all the milk and stir until the mixture leaves the sides of the bowl clean. Add remaining milk if necessary.

2. Turn it out onto a floured surface and knead quickly. Roll out to about 0.5-1.25cm/¼-½ inch thick, and cut the dough into rounds using a biscuit cutter.

3. Place the biscuit rounds on a greased baking sheet and bake in an oven preheated to 230°C/450°F/Gas Mark 8, for about 15 minutes, or until lightly browned and well puffed.

TIME: Preparation takes about 15 minutes and cooking takes 15 minutes.

SERVING IDEAS: Serve with cream cheese, or top with jam and cream.

SUNFLOWER CHOCOLATE COOKIES

These cookies come alive with the addition of sunflower seeds.

MAKES ABOUT 28

120g/4oz butter or margarine
120g/4oz light muscovado sugar
1 egg, beaten
1 tsp vanilla essence
½ tsp bicarbonate of soda
½ tsp salt
30g/1oz bran
90g/3oz rolled oats
120g/4oz wholemeal flour
60g/2oz sunflower seeds
120g/4oz chocolate drops

1. Beat together the butter and sugar until pale and creamy. Gradually add the egg, beating well after each addition.

2. Beat in the vanilla essence, then beat in the bicarbonate of soda, salt, bran, oats and flour mixing well until a stiff dough is produced. Finally, beat in the sunflower seeds and chocolate drops.

3. Place heaped spoonfuls of the mixture onto two greased baking sheets and bake for 5-10 minutes in an oven preheated to 190°C/375°F/Gas Mark 5.

4. Cool slightly on the tray then transfer to a wire rack to cool completely.

TIME: Preparation takes about 20 minutes, cooking time is about 10 minutes.

TO FREEZE: Form the dough into a 5cm/2-inch diameter block and freeze uncooked. When required, cut the required number of 6mm/¼-inch thick slices and bake as above.

SERVING IDEAS: Serve sprinkled with a little icing sugar.

SAND BISCUITS

These biscuits are lovely and rich despite their strange name which is a translation of the French word sablé.

MAKES 36

250g/9oz granulated sugar
225g/8oz butter
1 egg, beaten
225g/8oz plain flour
1 egg white, slightly beaten
Sugar
Finely chopped pecans or walnuts

---

1. Cream the sugar and butter together until light and fluffy.

2. Beat in the egg and gradually add the flour, working it in well to make a stiff dough. All the flour may not be needed.

3. Chill the mixture overnight, or until firm enough to roll out.

4. Roll out the dough in small portions on a well floured surface. Cut into 5-7.5cm/2-3 inch circles with a pastry cutter.

5. Place on greased baking sheets. Brush the tops with a little of the beaten egg white and sprinkle with a mixture of sugar and nuts.

6. Bake in an oven preheated to 180°C/350°F/Gas Mark 4, for about 10 minutes, or until crisp and pale golden.

7. Leave for a few minutes on the baking sheets then remove to wire cooling racks.

TIME: Preparation takes 20 minutes plus extra chilling time. Cooking takes about 10 minutes.

SERVING IDEAS: Sandwich two biscuits together using butter cream or jam for a special treat.

GINGER NUTS

These spicy biscuits are given a delicious texture by including nuts in the recipe.

MAKES 36

175g/6oz butter or vegetable margarine
120g/4oz dark muscovado sugar
120ml/4 fl oz golden syrup
2 tsps vinegar
3 eggs, beaten
2 tbsps milk
680g/1½lbs wholemeal flour
1½ tsps bicarbonate of soda
2 tsp ground ginger
½ tsp ground cinnamon
Pinch ground cloves
60g/2oz hazelnuts, chopped

1. Put the butter, sugar, golden syrup and vinegar into a bowl and beat well together until they are smooth and well blended.

2. Beat in the eggs and milk. Add the flour, soda, spices and hazelnuts, mixing well to form a firm dough.

3. Take small amounts of the biscuit mixture and roll into balls. Place well apart on two greased baking sheets. Press each biscuit down with a fork and bake for 5-10 minutes in an oven preheated to 190°C/375°F/Gas Mark 5.

4. Cool slightly on the tray then transfer to a wire rack to cool completely.

TIME: Preparation takes about 20 minutes, cooking time is about 10 minutes.

COOK'S TIP: If the syrup is difficult to measure out, warm the tin or jar by placing in a pan of warm water for a few minutes first.

PREPARATION: If the biscuit dough is too soft, add a little flour to firm it.

MUESLI COOKIES

These simple to make biscuits are full of wholesome ingredients.

MAKES ABOUT 36

120g/4oz butter or margarine
120g/4oz light muscovado sugar
1 egg, beaten
1 tsp vanilla essence
1 tsp baking powder
225g/8oz wholemeal flour
Pinch salt
120g/4oz sugarless muesli
60g/2oz currants

1. Beat together the butter and sugar until pale and creamy. Gradually add the egg, beating well after each addition. If the mixture starts to look curdled add 1 tbsp of the flour and beat in well.

2. Beat in the vanilla essence, then beat in the baking powder, flour, salt, muesli and currants to make a stiff dough.

3. Place heaped spoonfuls of the mixture on to two greased baking sheets and bake for 5-10 minutes in an oven preheated to 190°C/375°F/Gas Mark 5. Cool slightly on the tray then transfer to a wire rack to cool completely.

TIME: Preparation takes about 15 minutes, cooking time is about 20 minutes.

PREPARATION: If the dough is not stiff enough then add a little extra flour to make it firm enough to heap into piles.

SERVING IDEAS: Dip the cookies in melted chocolate.

TO FREEZE: This recipe can be frozen uncooked. Make a double batch, then cook as many biscuits as you need and freeze the remaining mixture in batches until required.

SPICED BISCUITS

Crunchy and wholesome, these spicy biscuits are a tea-time treat.

MAKES ABOUT 15 BISCUITS

120g/4oz wholewheat flour
½ tsp bicarbonate of soda
1 tsp ground cinnamon
1 tsp ground mixed spice
60g/2oz rolled oats
90g/3oz soft brown sugar
90g/3oz butter
1 tbsp golden syrup
1 tbsp milk

1. Put the flour, bicarbonate of soda, cinnamon, mixed spice, oats and sugar into a bowl and stir well to blend thoroughly. Make a well in the middle.

2. In a small saucepan, melt the butter with the syrup and milk over a gentle heat.

3. Pour the melted mixture into the dry ingredients and beat well, until the mixture forms a smooth and pliable dough.

4. Divide the mixture into about 15 small balls. Place these onto lightly greased baking sheets, keeping them spaced well apart, to allow the mixture to spread.

5. Flatten each ball slightly with the back of a wet spoon, and bake in a preheated oven at 180°C/350°F/Gas Mark 4, for about 15 minutes or until golden brown.

6. Allow the biscuits to cool on the baking sheet before removing them.

TIME: Preparation takes about 20 minutes, and cooking takes about 15 minutes.

VARIATION: Substitute ground ginger for the cinnamon and mixed spice.

COOK'S TIP: Heat a metal tablespoon, and use this to measure out the golden syrup, directly into the saucepan, to avoid a sticky mess.

OLD-STYLE MOLASSES COOKIES

The origins of American cookie recipes go back to the days of the Pilgrim Fathers.

MAKES ABOUT 45 COOKIES

150g/5oz sugar
175g/6oz molasses
150g/5oz butter
150ml/5 fl oz buttermilk
340g/12oz flour
1 tsp bicarbonate of soda
2 tsps cinnamon
1 tsp ginger
½ tsp cloves
½ tsp nutmeg
½ tsp salt
175g/6oz raisins

1. Place the sugar, molasses and butter in a large heavy-based saucepan and cook, stirring, until the mixture comes to the boil.

2. Allow it to boil for 1 minute, then remove from the heat and stir in the buttermilk.

3. Sift together the flour, bicarbonate of soda, spices and salt, and beat this thoroughly into the molasses mixture.

4. Chop the raisins, and stir them into the cookie mixture.

5. Drop teaspoonfuls of the mixture onto greased baking sheets, leaving plenty of space between them, and bake in an oven preheated to 180°C/350°F/Gas Mark 4, for 8-12 minutes.

6. When cooked, allow to cool slightly on the trays before removing to a cake rack to cool completely.

TIME: Preparation takes about 15 minutes and cooking takes 8-12 minutes.

COOK'S TIP: To make preparation easier, weigh the molasses directly into the saucepan.

SCOTTISH SHORTBREAD

Using rice flour gives the shortbread a good crisp texture.

MAKES 8 SLICES

120g/4oz butter
60g/2oz caster sugar
120g/4oz plain flour
60g/2oz rice flour

1. In a bowl, cream together the butter and sugar and add the sifted flours.

2. Using your fingers, lightly mix in all the ingredients until they change from a crumbly texture to a shortbread dough.

3. Roll or press out the dough with your fingers to a circle 5mm/¼-inch thick or press into a tin or shortbread mould. Prick the surface with a fork.

4. Bake in an oven preheated to 160°C/325°F/Gas Mark 3, for about 45-50 minutes or until pale golden.

5. Remove from the oven and mark out into wedges or fingers depending on tin or mould shape. Allow to cool in the tin or mould.

TIME: Preparation takes about 15 minutes and cooking takes 45-50 minutes.

COOK'S TIP: Store in an airtight tin.

BUYING GUIDE: Shortbread moulds can be bought from specialist kitchen shops.

CHOCOLATE FRUIT AND NUT COOKIES

Mixed fruit adds an extra dimension to these delicious cookies.

MAKES ABOUT 36

175g/6oz plain flour
¼ tsp baking powder
120g/4oz butter
175g/6oz demerara sugar
1 egg, beaten
Few drops vanilla essence
90g/3oz plain chocolate, coarsely chopped
60g/2oz almonds, chopped
60g/2oz walnuts, chopped
60g/2oz mixed dried fruit

1. Sift together the flour and baking powder.

2. In a bowl, cream together the butter and sugar until pale then add the beaten egg and vanilla essence.

3. With a metal spoon, gradually fold in the flour, followed by the chocolate, nuts and fruit.

4. Place generous teaspoons of the mixture onto greased baking sheets, leaving enough space between for the cookies to spread.

5. Bake in an oven preheated to 180°C/ 350°F/Gas Mark 4 for 15-20 minutes until golden brown and firm to the touch. Slide off the baking sheets onto wire cooling racks.

TIME: Preparation takes about 10 minutes and cooking takes 15-20 minutes.

PEANUT BUTTER BRAN COOKIES

These rich, crumbly cookies are just the thing for hungry children, mid-morning with a glass of milk.

MAKES ABOUT 35

120g/4oz butter or margarine
120g/4oz light muscovado sugar
1 egg, beaten
225g/8oz crunchy peanut butter
60g/2oz bran
120g/4oz wholemeal flour
Pinch salt
½ tsp baking powder
½ tsp vanilla essence

1. Beat together the butter and sugar until pale and creamy. Gradually add the egg, beating well after each addition.

2. Beat in the peanut butter, bran, flour, salt, baking powder and essence, mixing well to form a stiff dough.

3. Take small pieces of the dough and roll into balls. Place well apart on greased baking sheets and flatten slightly with a fork or palette knife.

4. Bake one tray at a time for 5-10 minutes in an oven preheated to 190°C/375°F/Gas Mark 5. Cool slightly on the tray then transfer to a wire rack to cool completely.

TIME: Preparation takes about 15 minutes, cooking time is about 10 minutes.

PREPARATION: If the biscuit dough is too soft, add a little extra flour.

PEAR AND APRICOT SLICE

Serve as a dessert, or for afternoon tea topped with thick Greek yogurt.

MAKES 8 SLICES

2 pears, approximately 340g/12oz
120g/4oz dried apricots, soaked
1 tbsp clear honey
2 tsps pear and apple spread
1 tbsp sunflower oil
1 egg
120g/4oz fine wholemeal flour
1 tsp baking powder
Flaked almonds, to decorate

1. Peel, core and chop the pears into small pieces.

2. Chop the apricots finely.

3. Mix together the honey, pear and apple spread, and stir into the pears and apricots.

4. Add the oil and egg and mix well.

5. Mix together the flour and baking powder and fold into the pear and apricot mixture.

6. Spread the mixture into a greased 15×20cm/6×8 inch tin.

7. Sprinkle with the flaked almonds.

8. Bake in a preheated oven at 190°C/375°F/Gas Mark 5, for about 25 minutes or until risen and golden.

9. Leave to cool and cut into 8 fingers.

TIME: Preparation takes about 15 minutes, cooking takes 25 minutes.

COOK'S TIP: Pear and Apple Spread is sugar free and can be bought at most health food stores. It is an ideal substitute for jam.

CHOCOLATE BROWNIES

These delectable chocolate bars with a fragile crusty top are a must for all chocaholics.

MAKES 9

90g/3oz plain flour
¼ tsp baking powder
Pinch salt
120g/4oz plain chocolate
60g/2oz butter
2 eggs
225g/8oz sugar
90g/3oz walnuts, chopped

1. Sift the flour, baking powder and salt together in a bowl.

2. Melt the chocolate and butter in a bowl over a small saucepan of hot water.

3. Beat the eggs with the sugar for 2 minutes until light and creamy.

4. Beat in the melted butter and chocolate, then fold in the flour and walnuts.

5. Grease and line a shallow 20cm/8-inch square tin and bake in an oven preheated to 160°C/325°F/Gas Mark 3, for 35 minutes. Cool in the tin and cut into squares.

TIME: Preparation takes about 25 minutes and cooking takes 35 minutes.

SERVING IDEA: Top with whipped cream or ice cream.

COOK'S TIP: Store in an air-tight container.

VARIATION: Use toasted chopped nuts.

CRANBERRY BARS

*Cranberries have a delicious flavour and are seldom used to their full potential.
This recipe certainly rectifies this and these delicious bars are sure to become a
firm family favourite.*

MAKES 12-16 BARS

120g/4oz butter or margarine
150g/5oz light muscovado sugar
120g/4oz plain flour, sieved
Pinch salt
90g/3oz rolled oats
120g/4oz cranberry sauce
60g/2oz walnuts, chopped

1. Put the butter or margarine and sugar in a bowl and beat together until thick and creamy. Stir in the flour, salt and oats and mix well.

2. Spread two-thirds of the mixture onto the base of a well greased 20.5cm/8-inch square baking tin, pressing down well.

3. Mix together the cranberry sauce and nuts and spread over the oat mixture. Crumble the remaining oat mixture over the top and spread out evenly with a knife.

4. Bake for 20 minutes in an oven preheated to 180°C/350°F/Gas Mark 4. Allow to cool for about 10 minutes, then mark into bars. Leave to cool completely in the tin before removing.

TIME: Preparation takes about 20 minutes, cooking time is about 20 minutes.

VARIATION: Try using your favourite jam in place of cranberry sauce.

CHOCOLATE BISCUIT CAKE

A very rich and delicious 'cake'.

MAKES 16 SQUARES

225g/8oz rich tea biscuits
120g/4oz butter
1 tbsp sugar
3 level tbsps cocoa powder
2 tbsps golden syrup
120g/4oz sultanas
175g/6oz plain chocolate

1. Place the biscuits in a thick plastic bag and break up into small pieces with a rolling pin. Place in a mixing bowl.

2. Put the butter, sugar, cocoa powder and syrup into a pan and melt over a low heat, stirring all the time.

3. Add to the biscuit crumbs together with the sultanas. Mix very thoroughly.

4. Press the mixture into a 20.3cm/8-inch square container.

5. Break the chocolate into a heatproof bowl, and place over a pan of simmering water until melted.

6. Cover the cake with the melted chocolate and mark it with the back of a fork.

7. Refrigerate until cold and set. Cut into squares and store in an airtight tin.

TIME: Preparation takes 20-25 minutes plus chilling time.

COOK'S TIP: Cut the cake with a heated knife to slice through the chocolate. Alternatively, melt 25g/¾oz of butter with the chocolate to give a softer topping.

VARIATION: Omit the sultanas.

Choc-Oat Slices

Perfect for the lunch box or a children's party.

MAKES 12 SLICES

120g/4oz plain chocolate
120g/4oz butter or block margarine
1 tbsp clear honey
225g/8oz porridge oats
120g/4oz sultanas
60g/2oz desiccated coconut

1. Break the chocolate into a pan and add the butter and honey.

2. Melt over a very low heat and stir until all the ingredients have melted.

3. Remove from the heat and add the oats, sultanas and coconut.

4. Spread the mixture evenly into a greased rectangular baking tin and bake in a preheated oven at 180°C/350°F/Gas Mark 4, for 25-30 minutes.

5. Cool slightly and cut into thin slices. When completely cold, remove and store in an airtight tin.

TIME: Preparation takes 10 minutes, cooking takes 25-30 minutes.

VARIATION: Raisins may be used in place of the sultanas. Try maple syrup instead of honey.

CINNAMON ALMOND SLICES

The combination of cinnamon with almond works perfectly in these tempting slices.

2 eggs
120g/4oz sugar
2 tbsps iced water
90g/3oz flour
1 tsp cinnamon
Pinch of salt
½ tsp baking powder
90g/3oz flaked almonds
Caster sugar

1. Beat the eggs and sugar together until light and fluffy, then beat in the iced water.

2. Sift the flour, cinnamon, salt and baking powder into the egg mixture. Add the almonds and mix thoroughly.

3. Pour the mixture into a well-greased square cake tin. Sprinkle the top with sugar.

4. Bake in an oven preheated to 180°C/350°F/Gas Mark 4, for about 25 minutes. Allow to cool, then cut into slices.

TIME: Preparation takes about 15 minutes and cooking takes 25 minutes.

VARIATION: Substitute allspice and hazelnuts for a different flavour.

Millionaires Shortbread

This recipe is an all time favourite and needs no introduction.

MAKES 15 BARS

Shortbread Base
120g/4oz butter
60g/2oz sugar
175g/6oz plain flour, sieved

Toffee Caramel
120g/4oz butter or margarine
60g/2oz sugar
2 tbsps golden syrup
140ml/¼ pint condensed milk

Chocolate Topping
120g/4oz plain chocolate
15g/½oz butter

1. For the shortbread base, cream the butter and sugar together until light and fluffy.

2. Add the flour and knead until smooth. Press the dough into a greased, 20.5cm/8-inch square shallow cake tin, and prick with a fork.

3. Bake in an oven preheated to 180°C/350°F/Gas Mark 4, for 25-30 minutes. Cool in the tin.

4. Put the ingredients for the toffee caramel into a small saucepan and stir until dissolved; bring slowly to the boil, and cook, stirring for 5-7 minutes.

5. Cool slightly, spread over the shortbread base in the tin and leave to set.

6. For the topping, melt the chocolate with the butter in a bowl over a small saucepan of hot water. Spread it carefully over the toffee, leave it to set then cut into fingers.

TIME: Preparation takes about 35 minutes and cooking takes 25-30 minutes.

WATCHPOINT: The water under the bowl of melting butter and chocolate should not boil, as the mixture will overheat.

HAZELNUT BROWNIES

These moist, cake-like brownies are an irresistable treat.

MAKES 16

120g/4oz butter or margarine
6oz light muscovado sugar
2 eggs
½ tsp vanilla essence
90g/3oz wholemeal flour
½ tsp baking powder
Pinch salt
60g/2oz hazelnuts, chopped
Icing sugar, to dust

1. Melt the butter and beat in the sugar, stirring until smooth. Gradually add the eggs and essence, beating well to prevent the mixture from curdling.

2. Stir in all the remaining ingredients except the icing sugar, mixing well to blend evenly.

3. Pour into a greased and lined 20.5cm/8-inch square cake tin. Bake in an oven preheated to 180°C/375°F/Gas Mark 5, for 25-30 minutes or until springy to the touch.

4. Allow to cool for 10 minutes in the tin, then turn out onto a wire rack to cool completely. Cut into 16 squares and dust with icing sugar before serving.

TIME: Preparation takes about 15 minutes, cooking time is about 30 minutes.

TO FREEZE: This recipe freezes well for up to 6 weeks.

ALMOND SLICES

Use your favourite jam to complement the tempting almond topping on these slices.

MAKES 16

Pastry Base
225g/8oz plain flour
¼ tsp salt
120g/4oz butter
Cold water to mix

Topping
60ml/4 tbsps jam
120g/4oz caster sugar
120g/4oz icing sugar
175g/6oz ground almonds
1 egg, plus 1 egg white
A few drops almond essence
30g/1oz flaked almonds, to decorate

1. Sift the flour and salt into a bowl and rub in the butter until it resembles fine breadcrumbs.

2. Add enough water to mix into a pliable dough.

3. Roll out the dough onto a floured surface and use to line a greased shallow 25×15cm/10×6 inch baking tin.

4. Pinch up the long edges to form a border. Cover the base with the jam.

5. In a clean bowl, mix together the sugars and almonds. Beat well and then add the whole egg, egg white and almond essence.

6. Use the almond mixture to cover the jam, spreading evenly with a knife. Sprinkle with almonds.

7. Bake in an oven preheated to 200°C/400°F/Gas Mark 6, for 20 minutes or until well risen and golden.

8. When cooked, cut into slices in the tin and leave to cool for 10 minutes. Remove and finish cooling on a wire rack.

TIME: Preparation takes 20 minutes and cooking takes about 20 minutes.

VARIATION: If wished, coat with a thin layer of glacé icing after cooling and then sprinkle on the almonds. Leave the icing to set before slicing.

CHOCOLATE MUESLI BARS

The oats in this recipe add a chewy texture to these tasty bars.

MAKES 12

120g/4oz butter or margarine
120g/4oz sugar
1 egg, beaten
Few drops vanilla essence
120g/4oz plain flour, sieved
½ tsp bicarbonate of soda
30g/1oz rolled oats
38g/5 tbsps cocoa powder, sieved

Chocolate Coating
120g/4oz plain chocolate, chopped or
    grated
15g/½oz butter

1. Beat the butter or margarine with the sugar until light and fluffy.

2. Beat in the egg, adding the essence, flour and bicarbonate of soda. Stir in the oats and the cocoa powder.

3. Spread the mixture onto a lightly greased baking tray, and mark out into bars with a knife.

4. Bake in an oven preheated to 190°C/375°F/Gas Mark 5, for 10-12 minutes or until lightly browned. Re-mark with a sharp knife and cool in one piece on a wire rack.

5. To make the chocolate coating, melt the chocolate and butter together in a bowl over a small saucepan of hot water, and pour evenly over the bars.

6. Separate the bars when set.

TIME: Preparation takes about 25 minutes and cooking takes 10-12 minutes.

COOK'S TIP: Store in an airtight tin.

CRUNCH

If kept for a couple of days the Crunch will become deliciously soft and sticky.

MAKES 24 SQUARES

225g/8oz butter or margarine
2 tbsps golden syrup
460g/1lb oats
225g/8oz soft brown sugar

1. Put the butter and syrup into a pan and melt gently over a low heat.

2. Place the oats into a large mixing bowl and mix in the sugar.

3. Pour the melted butter and syrup over the oats and mix well with a wooden spoon until evenly coated.

4. Put the mixture into a 30.5×20.3cm/ 12×8 inch Swiss roll tin and flatten well with the back of a spoon.

5. Bake in the centre of a preheated 180°C/350°F/Gas Mark 4 oven, for 30-35 minutes until golden brown on top.

6. Remove from the oven, allow to cool for 2-3 minutes then mark into squares.

7. Leave until nearly cold before removing from the tin. Store in an airtight container.

TIME: Preparation takes 10 minutes, cooking takes 30-35 minutes.

VARIATION: Use 275g/10oz of oats and 175g/6oz of unsweetened muesli.

CONTINENTAL GATEAU SLICES

An easy dessert that can be prepared a day or two in advance or frozen for future use. It is very rich, so serve in thin slices.

SERVES 8

120g/4oz butter
120g/4oz caster sugar
1 egg yolk
140ml/¼ pint milk
120g/4oz ground almonds
3 tsps coffee essence
120ml/4 fl oz medium sherry
2 packets sponge fingers (20 per packet)
Chopped nuts, to decorate

1. In a bowl, cream together the butter and sugar until light and fluffy, then gradually beat in the egg yolk and half the milk. Stir in ground almonds and coffee essence.

2. Pour the remaining milk and sherry onto a shallow plate. Dip the sponge fingers separately into this liquid and arrange a layer (approximately 7) on a long, flat dish.

3. Cover with a layer of the egg and sugar mixture. Repeat the dipped sponge layer, then completely cover the gateau with the remaining mixture.

4. Mask the sides with chopped nuts and decorate. Chill for several hours before serving.

TIME: Preparation takes about 25 minutes plus several hours chilling time.

PREPARATION: If wished, use a lined and greased loaf tin to layer up the gateau, reserving a little of the cream mixture to coat the sides with. Chill for several hours then turn out of the tin, coat the sides of the gateau with the reserved 'cream' and mask with the nuts.

CHOCOLATE PALMIERS

Adding chocolate to palmier biscuits makes them even more delicious.

MAKES 20

225g/8oz puff pastry
Icing sugar
90g/3oz plain chocolate, coarsely grated

To decorate
225ml/8 fl oz double cream, whipped
120g/4oz strawberries, sliced
Icing sugar, for dusting

1. Roll out the pastry, on a well-sugared surface, to a rectangle measuring approximately 30.5×25.5cm/12×10 inches.

2. Sprinkle with the chocolate and some sugar and press down with the rolling pin.

3. Take one of the shorter sides of the pastry and fold it over to the centre. Fold the opposite side over to nearly meet it at the centre. Sprinkle with more sugar and repeat the folding to make four layers. Fold one of the sections on to the other so that it is eight layers thick.

4. Cut into 5mm/¼-inch slices and place them cut side down on dampened baking trays. Space them well apart and flatten them a little.

5. Bake in an oven preheated to 220°C/425°F/Gas Mark 7, for 12-15 minutes, or until puffed and golden. Turn the palmiers over once they begin to brown.

6. Remove the palmiers from the trays with a palette knife and cool on a wire rack.

7. Whip the cream and use it to fill a piping bag fitted with a 1.25cm/½-inch rosette nozzle.

8. Shape swirls of cream on half of the palmiers and arrange the fruit on top of the cream.

9. Use the other palmiers to sandwich the fruit. Sprinkle with icing sugar and serve.

TIME: Preparation takes about 30 minutes and cooking takes 12-15 minutes.

VARIATION: Sprinkle with a little ground cinnamon when adding the chocolate to the pastry.

BAKLAVA

These Greek pastries are very buttery and rich, so serve them in small portions.

SERVES 6-8

Syrup
340g/12oz granulated sugar
90ml/6 tbsps liquid honey
340ml/12 fl oz water
1 tbsp lemon juice
1 tbsp orange flower water

Pastry
460g/1lb packet filo pastry
120g/4oz unsalted butter, melted
120g/4oz walnuts, almonds or pistachio
    nuts, chopped
1½ tbsps sugar
½ tsp ground cinnamon

1. First make the syrup by combining all the syrup ingredients in a heavy-based saucepan. Place over a low heat until the sugar dissolves, stirring occasionally.

2. Once the sugar is dissolved, raise the heat and allow the syrup to boil until it is thick enough to coat a spoon. This should take about 2 minutes. Allow the syrup to cool and then chill thoroughly.

3. Brush a 30×20cm/12×8 inch rectangular baking dish with some of the melted butter. Place about 8 of the pastry sheets in the dish, brushing the top of each with some of the melted butter.

4. Mix the nuts, sugar and cinnamon together and spread half of the mixture over the top of the pastry. Place two more layers of the buttered pastry on top and then cover with the remaining nuts. Layer up the remaining pastry, brushing each layer with butter.

5. With a sharp knife, score a diamond pattern in the top. Sprinkle the pastry with water to keep it moist and prevent curling.

6. Bake in an oven preheated to 180°C/350°F/Gas Mark 4, for 30 minutes and then raise the oven temperature to 220°C/425°F/Gas Mark 7. Continue baking for 10-15 minutes longer, or until the pastry is cooked and the top is golden brown and crisp.

7. Remove the pastry from the oven and immediately pour over the syrup. Leave the pastry to cool and when thoroughly cold, cut into diamond shapes to serve.

TIME: Preparation takes about 30 minutes, plus extra time for chilling the syrup. Cooking takes about 40-45 minutes.

COOK'S TIP: Baklava may be made several days in advance and kept in the refrigerator. Leave at room temperature for about 20 minutes before serving.

WATCHPOINT: When boiling the syrup, watch it constantly. Sugar syrups can turn to caramel very quickly. If this happens, discard the syrup and begin again.

FLORENTINES

Originally from Italy, as their name suggests, Florentines are a good accompaniment to a plain dessert, such as ice cream, but are just as tasty served with a cup of coffee at the end of a meal.

SERVES 4

175g/6oz sugar
2 tbsps honey
120ml/4 fl oz water
60ml/4 tbsps double cream
90g/3oz candied mixed peel
2 tbsps currants
30g/1oz flaked or slivered almonds
120g/4oz plain chocolate
60ml/4 tbsps milk

1. Place the sugar, honey and water into a saucepan and bring to a boil. Using a sugar thermometer, boil the syrup to 120°C/248°F then remove from the heat.

2. Pour in the cream and combine thoroughly.

3. Add the peel, currants and almonds and stir together well.

4. Form little patties of the mixture on a well greased baking tray. Cook each batch in a preheated oven at 200°C/400°F/Gas Mark 6, for about 10 minutes, or until the Florentines are golden brown.

5. Remove the biscuits from the oven and use a palette knife to scrape the cooked edges back towards the centres. Allow to cool for 2-3 minutes before removing them from the tray. Either cool on a rack or round a wooden rolling pin to give a curved shape.

6. In a bowl, melt the chocolate and milk together over a pan of hot water. Dip the Florentines into the chocolate mixture to coat half of each biscuit. Allow to harden and then serve.

TIME: Preparation takes about 20 minutes, cooking takes about 20 minutes.

WATCHPOINT: The Florentines bubble during cooking, but this stops once they have cooled down. Watch the biscuits carefully during cooking and do not let them overcook. Allowing the Florentines to cool before removing them from them from the tray is important; if they are too hot, they will fall apart.

POPPY SEED SLICES

This is the Christmas version of an ever popular Polish cake. As a symbol of holiday generosity, more poppy seeds were used than in the everyday recipe.

MAKES 2 ROLLS

Dough
175g/6oz butter or margarine
175g/6oz sugar
2 eggs
Pinch salt
90-120ml/3-4 fl oz milk
45g/1½oz fresh yeast
680g/1½lbs flour

Filling
420ml/¾ pint milk
225g/8oz black poppy seeds
90g/3oz butter or margarine
140ml/¼ pint honey
30g/4 tbsps walnuts, ground
90g/3oz raisins
2 tbsps finely chopped glacé peel
2 eggs
120g/4oz sugar
90ml/3 fl oz brandy

1. To prepare the dough, cream the butter with the sugar until light and fluffy and gradually add the eggs, beating well in between each addition. Add a pinch of salt and heat the milk until lukewarm. Dissolve the yeast in the milk and add to the other ingredients.

2. Sift in the flour and knead the dough until smooth and elastic. When kneading the dough, be sure to stretch it well and work on a lightly-floured surface. If necessary, flour your hands if the dough tends to stick.

3. To test if the dough has been sufficiently kneaded, press lightly with two fingers. If the dough springs back fairly quickly, it is ready to leave to rise.

4. Place the dough in a lightly greased bowl, cover with a damp cloth or lightly greased clingfilm and leave in a warm place for about 1 hour, or until doubled in bulk.

5. For the filling, bring the milk to the boil and mix with the poppy seeds. Cook over a low heat for about 30 minutes, stirring frequently. Drain the poppy seeds well and blend to a paste in a food processor or liquidizer.

6. Melt the butter and add the honey, walnuts, raisins and peel. Add the poppy seed paste and cook for about 15 minutes, stirring frequently over a moderate heat.

7. Beat the eggs with the sugar until light and fluffy, and combine with the poppy seed mixture. Cook over a gentle heat, stirring constantly until thickened. Add the brandy and set the filling aside.

8. When the dough has doubled in bulk, knock it back and knead for a further 2-5 minutes. Divide the dough in half. Roll each half out thinly on a floured surface, shaping into large rectangles.

9. Spread the filling evenly over each piece and roll up tightly as for a Swiss roll, pressing the ends together to seal. Place on a lightly buttered baking sheet, curving into horse shoe shapes.

10. Bake in a preheated 190°C/375°F/Gas Mark 5 oven for 45-50 minutes, or until golden brown. Cool, then cut into slices to serve.

SWEET YEAST BISCUITS

This recipe is from the Amish community in Pennsylvania, America. Although they are called biscuits they are in fact more like buns.

MAKES 12

910ml/1 pint 12 fl oz milk
4 eggs, beaten
60g/2oz butter, melted
25g/¾oz fresh yeast
120ml/4 fl oz lukewarm water
460g/1lb sugar
Flour

Topping
460g/1lb sugar
30g/4 tbsps flour
120g/4oz butter, softened
60ml/4 tbsps boiling water

1. Scald the milk and allow to cool slightly. Beat in the eggs gradually, along with the butter. Cool to lukewarm.

2. Mix the yeast and water and add to the milk mixture with the sugar and enough flour to make a thin batter. Cover and leave in a warm place overnight.

3. Add enough flour to the mixture to make a soft, pliable dough. Knead it lightly on a well-floured surface. Place in an oiled bowl and leave to rise again until doubled in size.

4. Knock out the air and knead again lightly. Roll out to 2.5cm/1-inch thick and cut out biscuit shapes. Place on an oiled baking sheet and leave to rise again until doubled in size.

5. Mix the topping ingredients to a smooth paste and brush over the tops of the biscuits.

6. Bake the biscuits in an oven preheated to 200°C/400°F/Gas Mark 6, for about 20 minutes, or until the bottoms sound hollow when tapped.

TIME: Preparation takes about 30 minutes excluding overnight standing and rising times. Cooking takes about 20 minutes.

VARIATION: If fresh yeast is unavailable use 1 sachet of dried yeast and continue as above. If wished substitute Quick Action dried yeast.

PRUNE, APRICOT AND NUT TORTE

This spectacular shortbread is ideal as the centrepiece for a sumptuous afternoon tea.

SERVES 6-8

120g/4oz dried apricots
120g/4oz dried prunes
280ml/½ pint red wine, or dry cider
120g/4oz wholemeal flour
120g/4oz butter or margarine
60g/2oz soft brown sugar
60g/2oz hazelnuts, freshly ground
3 tbsps finely chopped walnuts
2 tbsps clear honey, warmed
1 tbsp pine nuts
1 tbsp hazelnuts

---

1. Put the apricots and prunes into a large mixing bowl. Warm the wine, or cider, pour this over the dried fruits and leave them to stand for 4 hours, or until they are moist and plump.

2. Put the flour into a large bowl, and rub in the butter until the mixture resembles breadcrumbs.

3. Add the brown sugar, ground hazelnuts and the finely chopped walnuts to the flour mixture, and knead the mixture until it forms a soft dough.

4. Grease the base of a 21cm/8-inch fluted, loose-bottomed flan tin, and press the nut dough evenly into the tin.

5. Bake the dough in an oven preheated to 190°C/375°F/Gas Mark 5, for about 15 minutes.

6. Drain the prunes and apricots, and dry them thoroughly on kitchen paper.

7. Remove the shortbread from the oven, and arrange the soaked fruits in an attractive pattern over the top.

8. Cover with a piece of foil, and return the whole shortbread to the oven for a further 10 minutes.

9. Remove the shortbread from the oven, and allow it to cool for a few minutes in the tin, before removing it carefully and placing it on a wire rack to cool completely.

10. When the shortbread has cooled, transfer it to a serving plate, and glaze the top of the fruits with the warmed honey.

11. Sprinkle the pine nuts and the whole hazelnuts over the fruit, before serving.

TIME: Preparation takes about 30 minutes, plus 4 hours soaking time, and cooking takes about 25 minutes.

VARIATION: For a very subtle flavour use warm jasmine or orange blossom tea to soak the fruits in, instead of the wine or cider.

SERVING IDEAS: Serve the shortbread warm from the oven, instead of allowing it to cool.

COCONUT TILE COOKIES

These home-made cookies provide the perfect finishing touch to a wide variety of desserts and are particularly good as an accompaniment to ice creams or sherbets.

MAKES 30 COOKIES

120g/4oz sugar
2 egg whites
60g/2oz plain flour
60g/2oz melted butter
45g/1½oz desiccated coconut, ground
Extra butter for greasing

---

1. Beat the sugar into the egg whites.

2. Add the flour and butter, beating well. Beat in the coconut, then allow to rest for 10 minutes.

3. Butter baking trays. Use the back of a spoon to spread out 1 tbsp of batter for each cookie.

4. Cook each tray for 3-4 minutes in a preheated oven at 200°C/400°F/Gas Mark 6. Remove the cookies from the trays with a palette knife and immediately shape them around a rolling pin. They will cool and harden very quickly. Slide onto a wire rack to cool.

5. Repeat the cooking and cooling operation until all the cookie batter has been used up.

TIME: Preparation takes about 10 minutes and the complete cooking time takes about 35 minutes.

WATCHPOINT: Cooking time depends on the thickness of the cookies. As soon as they lightly colour around the edges, they are done.

VARIATION: The ground coconut can be replaced with ground almonds.

PRALINE ORANGE LOG

This makes a delightful and unusual tea-time treat.

MAKES 30 SLICES

175g/6oz plain chocolate, chopped or
  grated
1¼ tbsps strong black coffee
2 tbsps sugar
1¼ tbsps orange liqueur
175g/6oz butter
2 egg yolks

Praline
275g/10oz shelled nuts (see Cook's Tip)
225g/8oz granulated sugar
90ml/3 fl oz water
1 egg white, beaten

1. Melt the chocolate in a bowl with the coffee, sugar, orange liqueur and butter, over a small saucepan of hot water.

2. Remove from the heat and allow to cool thoroughly. Stir in the egg yolks. Chill for 3½-4 hours.

3. To make the praline; put the nuts on a baking sheet and warm them in an oven preheated to 180°C/350°F/Gas Mark 4, for 10 minutes. Butter a marble slab or large baking sheet.

4. Put the sugar and water into a small, heavy saucepan, stirring until the sugar has dissolved. Bring to the boil and boil until the sugar caramelizes; remove from the heat and plunge the base of the pan into cold water to halt the cooking process. Stir in the nuts.

5. Pour onto the marble or the baking sheet. Spread out and leave until set and hard. Put the praline into a strong plastic bag and crush with a rolling pin.

6. Shape the chilled chocolate mixture into a log, 2 inches in diameter. Brush the log with the beaten egg white and roll gently in the crushed praline, pressing firmly with the hands to help the praline stick.

7. Chill the log until very firm. Cut into slices about 5mm/¼-inch thick.

TIME: Preparation takes 20-25 minutes, plus chilling.

COOK'S TIP: Use either almonds, hazelnuts, walnuts or pistachio nuts for the Praline. Use the nuts chopped or whole, with or without the skins, toasted or plain. For praline powder, the nuts must be peeled.

MACAROONS

Perfect served with afternoon tea or with coffee at the end of a meal, these delicious little biscuits also make a good accompaniment to desserts of all kinds.

SERVES 6

2 egg whites
Salt
200g/7oz sugar
120g/4oz ground almonds

1. Beat the egg whites with a pinch of salt until foamy, then gradually add the sugar, beating continuously until the whites are stiff.

2. Fold the ground almonds into the egg whites to obtain a thick paste; the egg whites will lose some of their volume in the process.

3. Place the mixture in a piping bag fitted with a plain nozzle. Pipe small balls of paste onto baking sheets lined with buttered waxed paper, spacing them quite far apart. Do this in batches, if necessary.

4. Cook in an oven preheated to 180°C/350°F/Gas Mark 4, for 10 minutes or until lightly coloured. Remove from the oven and use a palette knife to transfer them to a cake rack to cool. Once cool, they become hard and crunchy.

TIME: Preparation takes about 15 minutes and cooking takes about 10 minutes per batch.

WATCHPOINT: Space the macaroons quite far apart on the sheets, as they spread during cooking.

Nut Tartlets

Use what ever nuts you like best – walnuts, pecans, even unsalted peanuts for these very moreish treats.

MAKES 12-16

Pastry
120g/4oz butter or margarine
90g/6 tbsps cream cheese
120g/4oz plain flour

Filling
90g/3oz chopped nuts
1 egg
175g/6oz light brown sugar
1 tbsp softened butter
5ml/1 tsp vanilla essence
Icing sugar

1. Beat the butter or margarine and cheese together to soften.

2. Stir in the flour, adding more if necessary to make the dough easy to handle, although it will still be soft. If possible, roll the dough into 2.5cm/1-inch balls. Chill thoroughly on a plate.

3. Mix all the filling ingredients together thoroughly, omitting the icing sugar.

4. Place a ball of chilled dough into a small individual patty tin and, with floured fingers, press up the sides and over the base of the tins. Repeat with all the balls of dough.

5. Spoon in the filling and bake for about 20-25 minutes in a preheated oven at 180°C/350°F/Gas Mark 4.

6. Allow to cool for about 5 minutes and remove carefully from the tins. Cool completely on a wire rack before sprinkling with icing sugar.

TIME: Preparation takes about 25 minutes. The dough will take at least 1 hour to chill thoroughly. Cooking takes about 20-25 minutes.

PREPARATION: If the dough is too soft to handle after mixing, chill for about 30 minutes or until easier to handle.

SERVING IDEAS: Serve with coffee or tea. The tartlets can be made in a larger size and served as a pudding with whipped cream.

LANGUES DE CHAT

*'Cat's tongues' are a classic accompaniment to ice cream or fruit desserts, and
are also traditionally served with afternoon tea.*

SERVES 6

165g/5½oz softened butter
250g/9oz icing sugar
1 tsp vanilla essence
5 egg whites
225g/8oz plain flour, sifted

1. Cream the butter with the icing sugar
and the vanilla essence until light and fluffy.

2. Add the egg whites one by one,
alternating with the flour until a firm dough
is obtained.

3. Place the dough into a piping bag fitted
with a plain nozzle. Pipe even-sized strips
of dough onto a greased baking tray. Leave
space between the biscuits as they spread
during baking.

4. Bake in preheated oven at 200°C/400°F/
Gas Mark 6, for 10-15 minutes: the edges
should be golden brown but the centres still
light.

5. When cooked, remove the biscuits from
the oven, allow them to cool slightly on the
baking tray, then use a spatula to lift them
onto a wire rack and leave to cool
completely.

TIME: Prepration takes about 15 minutes and cooking takes 10-15 minutes.

WATCHPOINT: Cooking time varies according to the size and thickness of
the bisuits; they are cooked when the edges are golden brown.

PALMIERS

Palmiers originated in France, where they can still be bought in pâtisseries all over the country. They make a perfect accompaniment to ice creams and sherbets or to fruit desserts.

SERVES 4

225g/8oz puff pastry
3 tbsps sugar
Icing sugar

1. Roll the puff pastry out to form a rectangle 30.5cm/12-inches wide.

2. Sprinkle a work surface with half the sugar.

3. Place the pastry on the sugared surface, and sprinkle over the remaining sugar. Roll lightly over the pastry so that the sugar sticks to it.

4. Fold each short side over to meet in the centre, and repeat to make four layers. Fold one folded section on top of the other so that there are eight layers. Place the rolled pastry in the freezer for 20 minutes to make it easier to slice.

5. Remove from the freezer and slice the rolled pastry into thin slices to form the palmiers.

6. Open the palmiers out a little and place the biscuits on a dampened baking tray. Bake in an oven preheated to 200°C/400°F/ Gas Mark 6, for 20 minutes or until golden brown.

7. Allow the palmiers to cool, then sprinkle with icing sugar before serving.

TIME: Preparation takes about 15 minutes, plus 20 minutes resting time. Cooking takes about 20 minutes.

COOK'S TIP: The palmiers should caramelise in the oven. Watch them carefully as they colour quickly.

PRALINE MILLEFEUILLE

This pastry makes a sophisticated accompaniment to tea or coffee.

MAKES 8

225ml/8 fl oz milk
1 tbsp praline powder (see Cook's Tip)
2 egg yolks
2½ tbsps sugar
1½ tbsps flour, sifted
340g/12oz puff pastry
Icing sugar
Cocoa powder

1. Bring the milk to the boil with the praline powder.

2. Beat together the egg yolks and the sugar until the mixture is light and lemon coloured. Beat in the flour, mixing well.

3. Pour the hot milk over the above mixture, combine well and pour back into the saucepan. Bring to a boil, then lower the heat and cook, stirring continuously, until the mixture thickens. Set aside to cool.

4. Roll the pastry out thinly into two rectangles, each measuring 30.5×20.5cm/12×8 inches. Prick the pastry well, trim edges and press onto dampened baking sheets. Cook above the centre of an oven preheated to 220°C/425°F/Gas Mark 7, and bake for 8-10 minutes, or until golden. Remove from the oven and allow to cool.

5. When the pastry has cooled, cut each rectangle in half lengthwise, to give four strips. Cut each strip crosswise into six, giving a total of twenty-four pieces.

6. Spread a little of the pastry cream onto one of the rectangles.

7. Cover the first rectangle with another puff pastry rectangle, spread over another layer of filling and finish with a third rectangle.

8. Continue to layer the pastry, to make eight finished pastries, each three layers thick. Sift a little icing sugar and cocoa over the top of the pastries to decorate.

TIME: Preparation takes about 35 minutes and cooking about 10 minutes.

COOK'S TIP: To make praline powder see recipe for Praline Orange Log and instead of crushing, grind the praline in a coffee grinder.

PREPARATION: Dampening the baking sheets with cold water creates steam to help the pastry rise.

HAZELNUT FLORENTINES

Hazelnuts make a good alternative to almonds in these crisp, toffee-like biscuits.
They're a treat with coffee or ice cream.

MAKES 24-30

460g/1lb shelled and peeled hazelnuts
225g/8oz sugar
90ml/6 tbsps honey
90ml/6 tbsps double cream
225g/8oz butter
175g/6oz white chocolate, melted
175g/6oz plain chocolate, melted

1. Place the hazelnuts in a plastic bag and tie securely. Tap nuts or roll them with a rolling pin to crush roughly.

2. Place the sugar, honey, cream and butter in a heavy-based saucepan and heat gently to dissolve the sugar. Bring to the boil and cook rapidly for about 1½ minutes. Remove from the heat and stir in the nuts.

3. Brush baking sheets well with oil and spoon or pour out mixture in even amounts. Make only about six Florentines at a time.

4. Bake for about 10 minutes in a preheated 190°C/375°F/Gas Mark 5 oven. Allow to cool on the baking sheets and, when nearly set, loosen with a palette knife and transfer to a flat surface to cool completely.

5. When all Florentines have been baked and cooled, melt both types of chocolate separately. Spread white chocolate on half of the Florentines and dark chocolate on the other half, or marble the two if preferred.

6. Place the biscuits chocolate side uppermost to cool slightly and then make a wavy pattern with the tines of a fork, or swirl the chocolate with a knife until it sets in the desired pattern.

TIME: Preparation takes about 45-50 minutes and cooking takes about 10 minutes per batch.

TO FREEZE: Store well wrapped for up to 1 month. Unwrap and defrost, chocolate side up, at room temperature. Store in a cool place.

SERVING IDEAS: Make in small sizes, about 2-2.5cm/1½-2 inches, for petit fours.

Index